A LITTLE SPT OF BELONGING

To my children, Ryan and Anna.

This book BELONGS to:

_____

_____

_____

Hi, I'm a little SPOT of BELONGING.

BELONGING is a FEELING you get when you have a great friend, when you are part of a group, or when you are part of a community that supports you. It is also a FEELING of CONFIDENCE and loving who you are!

Every human on this planet wants to FEEL like they BELONG, and we all have the power to help each other feel that way!

You might already FEEL like you BELONG somewhere!

Like a...

FAMILY

CLUB

BAND

TEAM

SCHOOL

There are so many places

where you can BELONG!

When you BELONG, you FEEL
VALUED, SAFE,
CALM, and
ACCEPTED.

Those are amazing FEELINGS!

Did you know you can help others FEEL like
they BELONG, too?

You can do this by showing KINDNESS!

It's easy to show KINDNESS!

For example, you could ask someone to play!

Invite someone to a party.

Share your things.

Lend a hand when someone needs help.

I'm here to help everyone feel like they BELONG!

Because when you FEEL like you
DON'T BELONG, you can FEEL

LONELY,
SCARED, and
ANGRY.

NOT BELONGING is when you FEEL left out or excluded. It's the FEELING you get when you think that kids don't like you.

That's why BELONGING needs to start with you, first!

It's important to like yourself,
believe in yourself, and care for yourself.

You are
amazing!

When you start to do that, making friends becomes a lot easier.

For example, CONFIDENCE can show when you SMILE.

SMILING can show someone that you are friendly.

Now, if you pair a SMILE with introducing yourself, you will be on your way to making friends in no time!

I like to use...Hi, My name is...

Asking questions is another great way to show someone that you want to be their friend. When you ask questions, it gives you a chance to build a connection. You might even find something in common!

I made this chart to give you some ideas of what to ask.

CONVERSATIONS can be a little tricky sometimes because they require **TEAMWORK**.

Think of a CONVERSATION like a game of catch.

When the ball is tossed, ask a question. Like, "What did you do this weekend?"

When the ball is caught, answer the question. Like, "I went to the park!"

Now TOSS the ball back and ask a question. Like, "What did YOU do this weekend?"

When the ball is caught, answer the question. Like, "I went swimming."

Let's PRACTICE!

What's your favorite food?

I like pizza!

I like pizza, too!

Another essential part of BELONGING is making sure everyone is included. So, if you see someone standing alone nearby, ask them to join you.

Including others can make things more fun.
It is also a great way to make NEW friends!

Sometimes you might want to BELONG so badly that when you see a friend making a BAD choice, you might feel the need to join in, too.

Instead, of joining in, you should say something to stop it. Having the courage to stand up for what is right is the better choice.

I know we covered a lot, and there is still so much to learn.

If we ALL practice being KIND to ourselves and others,
one day everyone in this world will feel like they

BELONG!

You can find this printable along with lesson plans and other fun activities on www.dianealber.com

Get to know you BINGO!

Do you have a dog?	Do you like pizza?	Do you like to read?	Do you like to write?
Do you like to ride a bike?	Do you like to paint?	Do you like dinosaurs?	Do you like to sing?
Do you like to play soccer?	Do you like to play chess?	Do you like to dance?	Do you like to bake?
Do you like to build a rock pile?	Do you like unicorns?	Do you like apples?	Do you like to draw?
Do you like to play baseball?	Do you like to play video games?	Do you have a cat?	Do you like to play music?

65864515R00020